Order this book online at www.trafford.com
or email orders@trafford.com

Most Trafford titles are also available at major online book retailers.

© Copyright 2019 Chance Hansen & Pascha Hansen.

All rights reserved. No part of this publication may be reproduced, stored in a retrieval system, or transmitted, in any form or by any means, electronic, mechanical, photocopying, recording, or otherwise, without the written prior permission of the author.

Print information available on the last page.

ISBN: 978-1-4907-9717-5 (sc)
ISBN: 978-1-4907-9718-2 (hc)
ISBN: 978-1-4907-9719-9 (e)

Library of Congress Control Number: 2019913462

Because of the dynamic nature of the Internet, any web addresses or links contained in this book may have changed since publication and may no longer be valid. The views expressed in this work are solely those of the author and do not necessarily reflect the views of the publisher, and the publisher hereby disclaims any responsibility for them.

Any people depicted in stock imagery provided by Getty Images are models, and such images are being used for illustrative purposes only. Certain stock imagery © Getty Images.

Trafford rev. 09/19/2019

North America & international
toll-free: 1 888 232 4444 (USA & Canada)
fax: 812 355 4082

Thank You

To YHVH for giving me the ability and talent to create stories, Pascha Hansen for all the amazing illustrations—you make these books come to life—and Granny and Grandad for all your help and support.

To Jill for the coffee and for letting us spend so many hours writing and illustrating at the Cookhouse on Main in Sangudo and to Perks Coffee House in Spruce Grove for the hours of writing and illustrating we accomplished there to.

To all the readers out there, you guys are awesome!

CHAPTER 1

Staring at his shelves of books, Captain Bacon pulled out his ship's log. Taking a deep breath, he dropped it on his desk before pulling a chicken feather pen and a bottle of ink closer to his work area. Sitting down at his chair, he took in a deep breath. The pirate captain listened quietly for the slightest oink from outside. The slightest disturbance could distract him from this very important work. He smiled at the sound of nothingness—complete silence apart from the gentle rocking of the ship. It was calm enough to fall asleep or go mad from boredom. Pulling the chicken feather pen out of the jar of ink, he hovered the quill above the blank page in the book. Just as he placed the pen on the paper, an earth-shattering shake rattled the picture frames and the rusty door to the captain's quarters. Captain Bacon looked up at the door as a huge blotch of ink dripped onto the fresh page. Angrily, Captain Bacon threw the pen on the book before storming outside into the bright sunshine.

"What is the meaning of this?" he shouted as he looked around, not seeing anyone on deck.

He grabbed the door frame to steady himself as another earthshattering boom vibrated under his hoof. Walking across the deck, he went toward the door to the lower decks. At the top of the stairs,

he stepped on a slippery banana peel. His hoof swung out from under him as his rump thumped down every step all the way to the pigpen.

"What on the Albatross Sea is the ruckus about?" he demanded as soon as he landed at the bottom of the stairs.

Everyone looked over from their ham-mocks. "You fell down the stairs." A large hairy boar looked at the captain.

Captain Bacon glared at him, annoyed. "No. I mean, earlier, Tusk. Who was banging around in the pigpen?"

"That rumble came from the belly of the ship," Curly said.

An uneasy silence filled the air as the captain looked around for a different excuse.

"Maybe the ship's hungry?" Pickles replied.

Captain Bacon glanced behind Tusk, seeing Pickles lying in a ham-mock, relaxing. "Pickles! What are you doing, and what's with the hammer?"

Pickles looked over at the captain. "I am resting, Captain. We haven't raided anything for seven days, and I am preparing for a big attack. I sleep with a hammer since Curly ate Buttons, my teddy."

The captain grunted in disbelief. "Very well. As long as you don't disturb me. I better not hear you hammering in the morning or in the evening. I don't want any disruptions while I work on it."

"Don't worry, Captain. If you hear me, I'll use it to hammer out a warning," Pickles assured.

"Don't make me pull your pork," Captain Bacon said warningly as he stared at Pickles wondering how to take his assurances before heading up the stairs into his quarters.

Sitting down at his desk, he looked at the book and the big blob of black ink sitting on the top of the page. He let out a frustrated grunt.

Grabbing the page, he tore it out of the book. A similar black blob of ink sat on the next page. Tearing out the next page revealed another ink stain on the third page. Grabbing the entire ship's log, he tossed it into the horn-shaped garbage can.

Turning around, he pulled a book off the bookshelf. Opening it to the first blank page, he pulled his chicken feather pen and ink jar closer to his workspace.

Bacon's Log

It has been a week since we've seen another ship, and I fear Pickles is plotting some dastardly plot against one of my crew, probably against Sausage up in the boar's nest. Don't ask me what issue the two of them have against each other, but Pickles is always plotting against that runt. There is something about those two always butting snouts, especially on slow days like this. I know I should be out there keeping an eye on Pickles, but this is quite an important responsibility.

Suddenly, a knock came from the closed door.

"I told you I do not wish to be disturbed!" the captain shouted.

Slowly, the door opened anyway.

Closing Bacon's Log, Captain Bacon looked up, seeing his first mate Truffles rush in.

"Captain Bacon!" Truffles looked down. "Did I disrupt you when you were writing in your diary?"

"It is not a diary! It is a ship's log. I keep facts and stories in it containing the crew, myself, and what happens. What are you doing in my pen anyway?"

"Sausage has spotted a chicken freighter off the port bow!" Truffles said, walking up to him.

Captain Bacon grinned because nothing was more important to Captain Bacon than eggs.

"We must turn toward that ship and keep all hooves off deck until we are closer—we have a ship to raid. Oh, and see to it that the *Squealer* goes steady and slow. Remember, the clucks are most timid and run if they sense any danger. I will be out shortly for a peep."

"Yes, Captain," Truffles said before stepping out.

"One more thing," he said before Truffles could close the door. "Keep an eye on Sausage and Pickles. I feel some trouble brewing between them."

"I will, Captain," Truffles said surely.

As he was about to close the door to his pen, the captain spoke up one last time.

"See to it that Sausage gets an egg flag waving on the mast."

"I will, Captain," Truffles said, holding the door open. "Is that all, sir?"

"Yes! Get out now!" Captain Bacon said, opening his captain's log.

"Yes, sir," his first mate said before slamming the door quickly.

The moment the door banged shut, all the pictures of past captains fell to the floor. Looking up from his log, he noticed all the nails were missing from the wall.

"PIIIICKLES!" Captain Bacon shouted, frustrated.

Dropping the pen, he walked over and gathered the pictures of the *Squealer*'s previous captains off the floor.

I'm never going to get all my writing done, he thought before placing them in a drawer in his desk. *I'll get some nails and snatch Pickles's hammer later,* he thought, looking over his desk.

He groaned, seeing a huge ink stain on the page. Pulling his pen off the page, he tossed the book in the garbage can. Pulling another new book off his shelf, half of the shelves crashed to the floor. *How and why is he taking off with all these nails?* he wondered as he began neatly stacking the books on the floor around his desk.

Bacon's Log

I've got a prepared Pickles prank problem. First off, I have no idea how he pulls them off. Like last time, he really had me going. I guess you wouldn't know since this is my first entry. Let me just fill you in.

Pickles decided to convince the crew he was a magic pig that could predict the future if he shoved his head in a barrel of water. He wasn't all that good, but I allowed him to have his fun. That is until we all realized our entire supply of apples disappeared. It turns out, it was an apple barrel that he filled with water, and whenever he dunked his head into the water, he would take off with an apple. None of us were very happy when the entire ship was empty to the core.

I am wondering how he was able to keep the pictures on the wall without nails. It's like physics don't apply to him. If I could actually catch him doing something, I could actually make a just punishment, but no one seems to ever see him doing anything.

Apart from the "Pickled" prank problem, a lot more has happened.

My first mate Truffles has been keeping an ear to the sky, an eye on the horizon, and his snout to the ground in search for unsuspecting ships and most importantly on my crew. It is great to have a trusted first mate to keep an eye on the crew when you're too busy. And as captain, it does feel great to give my chores to someone else when I don't feel like doing them. Truffles said Sausage has spotted a chicken freighter in the distance. We must approach slowly and stealthily. Those cluck ships are fast, and they're frightened easily. If they figure out our intent before we close in, there is a chance that they will escape. Some of my crew is crafty and troublesome, but others are clueless and tend to cause mistakes. It was quite embarrassing. You see, last time, it was the month of Oats. My crew and I were creeping up to a chicken freighter. We hadn't made a sound, and we were close enough to hear the rooster crow. That's when Slim sneezed. He had an unfortunate allergy to chicken feathers, and when he sneezed, it alerted the feathered crew, which made them turn tail and run. We didn't give up though. We decided to chase the chicken. Unfortunately, the chicken run didn't last long, and we were really out of reach.

It has been quite quiet since Slim retired to New Hampton, New York. I do wonder how he is doing in that little hamlet of a town.

Unfortunately, where chickens lack in intelligence, they make up in speed and acute hearing.

Strangely enough, the day Slim left, he warned me about a ship with tattered sails. He never said what the ship contained, but his warning was clear that it struck fear in every pig pirate that sails.

PLUNGER

CHAPTER 2

He thoughtfully stopped writing. What did chicken freighters have down in the hold? Looking over his shoulder, he saw his dictionary sitting on the bookshelf. Groaning, Captain Bacon leaned back, nearly falling over. A slight wave shifted the ship. Captain Bacon squealed, falling with a thud, his head hit the base of the bookshelf.

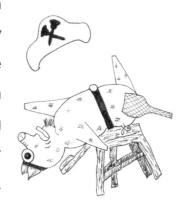

Gasping, he watched as the dictionary slipped off the shelf, landing on his head.

Lifting the book off his face, he chuckled as he stared at the information he wanted. The book opened to the exact page he needed.

Peep Ship's Information.
How to identify: Oval egg flag, sleek, and built for speed
Ship's advantage: Fastest
Best way of approach: Slow and quiet
Possible inventory: eggs, feathers, padding, pillows, diapers, paper

Captain Bacon closed the dictionary before closing the journal and locking it in his large desk. Stepping outside, he put on his pirate hat, hiding his shinny pink bald head.

"What's our speed, Truffles?" Captain Bacon asked the hog at the helm.

"We are going three nautical miles an hour."

"Please speak English, Truffles. About how long until we reach the roost?"

"We will reach the ship within about two hours, Captain."

"Perfect. I will prepare the crew below deck," Captain Bacon said.

Looking up in the boar's nest, Sausage was hanging by his hoof over the nest. He had the flags gripped in his front hooves. The egg and plunger flags waved together in the wind.

"What are you doing?" Captain Bacon shouted up to the upside-down pig scout.

"Apart from hanging around, sir, I'm trying to attach the egg in our flag's place, but I got caught up in the ropes, and now I'm dangling by a ham-string."

"Stay up there in the nest. I need someone to sit up there and keep an eye on that ship and take down that plunger flag. I want to get in nice and close before they decide to escape. It better be down before I come back—no excuses," Captain Bacon ordered before opening the door.

"Yes, Captain," the skinny pig said.

Captain Bacon looked around the stairs for banana peels before stepping down them.

"Woah!" Captain Bacon ducked as an apple shot over his head, knocking off his hat.

The sunlight shone off his head like a lighthouse. Ducking for his hat, he threw it on, hoping the shine from his head wasn't noticed by the ship. The apple sailed through the air, hitting the rope attached to Sausage's hoof.

"Who's rocking the rope?" Sausage shouted as he began to swing around the nest. "Don't worry about me, Captain, I'll find a way up sooner or later," Sausage said.

Suddenly, the rope on Sausage's hoof untied. Captain Bacon covered his eyes with his hooves. *SPLASH!* Captain Bacon removed his hooves from his eyes to see a huge wave hit him, knocking him off his hoof. Captain Bacon looked down at his drenched clothes from his seated position on the deck.

"I'm all right!" Sausage called, spitting out water. "The water broke my fall."

"Well, I'm not. You soaked my best pirate costume!" Captain Bacon shouted, placing his soggy hat back on his head. "Just get back up there and change that flag."

Shaking his head, Captain Bacon turned around as a second apple flew toward him. Gasping in shock, the apple hit him in the mouth. Stepping backward, he tripped

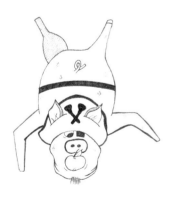

on the step above him before falling all the way

down the stairs. *Thud, thud, thud!* A massive elastic band was about waist high across the stairs. A pail of apples sat near the wall. Captain Bacon looked around from the base of the stairs, seeing everyone looking at him, everyone but Pickles who was sleeping in one of the ham-mocks. Spitting out the apple onto the floor, Captain Bacon looked at his crew angrily.

"Who was it that set up that contraption to hit me with apples?"

Taking a step toward Pickles rocking in the ham-mock, Captain Bacon stepped on the apple. Tripping on it, he flew forward. Arms outstretched, Captain Bacon grabbed the edge on his ham-mock to keep steady.

"Hey!" Pickles shouted as the captain fell to the floor.

"OOOF!" Captain Bacon groaned as Pickles landed on his

back. "Get off my back, relish for brains!" the captain shouted.

Pickles jumped off their leader.

Captain Bacon lay there, unmoving.

"Help me up!" he shouted. "I think Pickles jarred my back!" he said as Tusk held out a hoof.

"What is going on?" Curly asked as he clumped up from the mess hall.

"Apart from being crushed by the Pickler, there's a brood ship on the horizon," Captain Bacon said.

Tusk hopped from one hoof to the other excitedly.

"It's so great!" Tusk cheered. "I haven't been this excited since the last time we almost caught a ship. Unlike that time, I feel like we will win and get some amazing supplies. Have you ever realized that the word 'supplies' contains 'lies'? How can stuff be untruthful? Oh! Maybe it's because it's more like an unmoving rest like Curly on a Tuesday. Did you know that Curly—?"

"Silence, Tusk," Captain Bacon ordered. "We will be in invading range within an hour and a half."

All his crew looked at their leader.

"Prepare for an attack, but be quiet about it. I don't want to lose that ship like we did when Slim was on our crew," he said before turning and walking up the wooden stairs.

Clump! Thump! Clump Thump! His pig leg and peg leg thumped up the stairs as Captain Bacon headed back on deck, greeting Truffles. "Do we have any clue as to which chicken freighter it is?"

"Not from here but perhaps Sausage."

Pulling a sling shot from his belt, Captain Bacon fired a pebble, hitting the base of the boar's nest. A squeal of surprise came from Sausage. Suddenly, the little pig with a mop of hair looked over his nest at Captain Bacon.

"Yes, Captain," Sausage called down.

"What is the name of the ship we are approaching?"

"One moment, sir," Sausage said, looking toward the ship through a spyglass. "It's too far to tell, Captain."

"Look through the other side," Captain Bacon muttered to himself.

After a moment, Sausage flipped the spyglass around. "I can see it is a chicken ship, Captain."

"They're not called a ship, it's called a freighter!" the captain shouted back. "And I know that already. What is the name on the side?"

"It's called . . . *Beaker!*"

"Remember, Sausage, if you see a ship with tattered sails, let me know the minute you see it," Captain Bacon reminded Sausage. "Well, *Beaker*, it is time to face the *Squealer*," he said menacingly to himself.

Tusk the boar warrior appeared with a plunger in hand as he saluted Captain Bacon on the deck. The rest of the sounder crew below deck are prepared to plunger and plunder the chicken freighter.

"Perfect!" Captain Bacon squealed with joy as he rubbed his hooves together. "Go below deck and prepare the cannon on the port bow. I will let you know when we are within plunger range."

Slowly, the *Squealer* ship came closer and closer to the *Beaker*.

"Captain, if we wait any longer, I'm sure they'll figure out our intentions and fly the coop."

Looking over the bannister, Captain Bacon counted down in his head, *Five, four, three* . . .

He stared at the ship, and the chickens walking around the deck far above them.

Two, one. "NOW!" Captain Bacon shouted as loud as he could.

BANG! The sound of a cannon being fired echoed through the air.

Captain Bacon watched as a giant plunger with a huge

rope sailed through the air before sticking the side of Beaker's starboard side. They were attached to the Beaker. There was no way for them to escape the suction of Captain Bacon's plungers.

"ATTACK!" he shouted as about a dozen plungers tied with ropes sailed through the air, sticking to parts of the peeps' ship.

Taking a bow, Captain Bacon aimed his plunger and fired at the ship. He watched as the plunger sailed through the air, hitting the mast, before he started climbing the rope. Making it up the rope, he collapsed onto the deck of the chicken freighter, gasping for breath and out of energy. Captain Bacon looked to see most of the invasion was finished as most of the cluck crew was either cornered or plungered. *My crew are quite impressive. They overtook the ship in the time that it takes me to climb all the way up here. Best crew ever.*

"What is the meaning of this?" an old rooster shouted, opening the door to the captain's quarters.

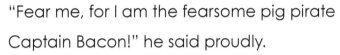

Captain Bacon approached the rooster, a plunger in one hoof.

"Fear me, for I am the fearsome pig pirate Captain Bacon!" he said proudly.

"Wrapped in bacon? I've never heard of you, but clearly, it fits you," the old rooster said plainly.

Some of the sounder crew chuckled at his comment.

"Silence, swine!" Captain Bacon shouted before turning back to the *Beaker*'s leader.

"I am Captain Bacon, leader of the pig pirates. I am not wrapped in bacon!" he shouted angrily.

"OH! Captain Bacon! I thought you said 'wrapped in bacon.' You see, my hearing isn't so well since—"

"Silence! I don't need to hear your medical history. I just want what is down in the nest. Tell me, what do you have, anything down in the egg carton?"

"Why, you dirty rotten pigs! You're here to get your wormy hooves on my diapers! You will never get away with it! Captain Bacon! I, Captain Sanders, will see to that."

"I think I already have," Captain Bacon snorted. "Your ship and crew have been plungered." The pig captain laughed. *Har! Snort! Harg!* "Pickles! Tusk! Go down into the henhouse and see what treasure this crew has," Captain Bacon ordered before facing Captain Sanders. "Now tell me, you chubby chicken, what do you think I want to see on your ship?"

Captain Sanders looked at the ruthless pigs. "I'm sure you don't care what you find, but you may not be pleased."

Suddenly, Pickles and Tusk, covered in feathers, came back on deck. "There are probably four thousand diapers and nine hundred pounds of paper."

"What? No eggs!" Captain Bacon shouted.

"No eggs," Tusk said sadly, spitting out a mouthful of white feathers.

"What was that? You are looking for eggs, lard breath?" Captain Sanders shouted.

"Yes! Wait, what?" Captain Bacon shouted. "Was that supposed to be a fat crack, or is it because I'm a pig you think I'm filled with lard?"

"You're the pudgy piggy, not me," Captain Sanders crowed.

Captain Bacon turned a fried shade of red. "Because of that insult, I'm taking double of what I intended to take. I am looking for anything to take, but eggs are the most important," Captain Bacon snarled back. "You think you can make a fool out of me? Tusk, Curly, Pickles, take the paper and a thousand diapers. We are not leaving this ship empty-handed."

"I didn't expect you to leave without taking something, Captain, but this is pathetic. It's not like you can make chicken scratch on paper," Curly complained.

"You don't need to care about what I'm going to do with the stuff. But since you asked, let me tell you . . . With paper, we can make many prints—hoof prints, that is. And don't you know, every captain needs to write in a book? Besides, I have been having some journal trouble and having extra paper to write on never hurts." Bacon then turned his attention from Curly back to the head rooster. "There is still one thing bothering me. Why don't you have any eggs? I thought all cluck ships carried eggs. For feathered folk like you, eggs are what pays your crew."

"Oh. The reason I don't have a single egg is because I'm retiring after this shipment. You see, this time I'm not doing it for the money. I'm doing it as a final journey," Captain Sanders clucked.

"Captain Bacon stared at him in amazement. "You aren't sailing for money? That doesn't make sense!"

"Of course, it won't make sense to a greedy pig like you."

"Excuse me, you old crow! I should tweak your beak for saying that!" Captain Bacon squealed. He watched as his potbellied crew tossed diapers and paper onto his ship. "Until next time, fried friend," Captain Bacon called to Captain Sanders.

"You will never get away with this, you Bacon hog, or my name isn't Eggbert Sanders Jr.!" he shouted toward the *Squealer*.

"Silence, drumstick. Until we meet again. You just witnessed the attack of the dreaded Bacon thief." "Captain," Tusk spoke up to their leader.

"Yes?" he responded, annoyed for getting his cheer interrupted.

"Permission to go below deck and have a hog wash to get all these itchy chicken feathers off?"

"Only after our victory cheer," Captain Bacon said annoyed before turning his attention back to the *Beaker*.

The captain and his crew squealed with joy as they left *Beaker* to find more ships to raid.

CHAPTER 3

> Bacon's Log
>
> Today we have raided an old rooster named—

aptain Bacon had to think for a minute. *What was his name? Why can't I ever remember the names of anyone I raid?*

> Today we have raided an old rooster. Our low-sailing sneak attack was no match for the ship called *Beaker*. Even Tusk is enjoying our saddest victory yet.

> Honestly, who on the Albatross Sea takes a cheap inventory of something like diapers?
> By the way, did you know all he had was paper and diapers? That's insane! Who needs hundreds of pounds of diapers and paper? It was too much for us to take, but we took enough for . . . Well, honestly, I haven't figured out what we are going to use them for yet.

Captain Bacon looked up, hearing a knock on his door.

"What is it?"

Truffles walked in. "I hate to interrupt you after a successful raid, especially when writing it down in your diary, but—"

"It is a ship's log, not a diary. There is a difference," Captain Bacon said defensively. "In a ship's log, the captain writes his hopes, dreams, fears about the future, the crew, and what happens throughout a day."

"Isn't that what you do with a diary?" Truffles asked.

"Forget about the diary—no, I mean log," Captain Bacon corrected himself. "Why did you come in here in the first place?"

"Curly spotted another ship on the horizon."

"Another ship? Are you sure he isn't looking at the *Beaker*?"

"He is sure, sir. It's wider and looks tougher."

"How is that possible? We never find two ships out in the same area within an hour." After a thoughtful moment, Captain Bacon gave a crafty grin. "We shall go forward!"

Stepping away from his desk, Captain Bacon took a spyglass off his large desk before going toward the starboard side of the ship in search for the next Bacon victim.

"I don't see it. Perhaps it's too small to bother even raiding."

"Sir?"

"What is it, Truffles?" he asked, not looking away from the horizon.

"The ship is on the port bow."

"Oh yes, of course." Captain Bacon nodded before heading to the other side of the ship. "I knew that," Captain Bacon said before searching the other horizon, spotting a ship out in the distance. "Heh! From this distance, the ship seems small. I wonder how large the ship really is. Then again, our ship is no more than eighteen snouts above the calm waves of the Albatross Sea. That's why it's such a stealthy ship. We are mostly sunk already."

"I know, Captain. You often remind me every time we lose a ship."

Ignoring his first mate, Captain Bacon turned toward the boar's nest.

"Sausage!" Captain Bacon called.

"I believe he is fast asleep again," Truffles informed the captain.

Pulling out his slingshot, Bacon fired a pebble at the lookout.

Squealing, Sausage looked over the edge. "Yes, Captain." Sausage grunted.

"Keep an eye on that ship and alert us the moment you know what it is called."

"Aye, Captain."

"Set a course toward that ship," Captain Bacon told Truffles.

"Yes, sir."

"Captain!" Sausage called from above.

"What is it?"

"It's the ship. The one on the horizon seems no larger than the ship we raided. Up close, it can't be much larger than a rowboat!"

Captain Bacon stood staring at him for a minute before shouting back, "Sausage, don't you know a ship gets larger the closer you get to it?"

"Aren't you sure it doesn't get smaller?"

Captain Bacon turned to Truffles, asking, "How did he become such a clueless piglet, and why is he part of my crew?"

"He was always a clueless piglet. You liked his ambition and his desire to follow your orders."

"I see," Captain Bacon said, scratching his chinny-chin chin. "Perhaps he could be useful somewhere else."

"He fell off the deck all the time. This so-called curse that he claims to have seems to haunt him whenever he leaves the boar's nest. You can look it up in your diary—err, bacon logs."

"There's no such thing as curses. He probably didn't become a sea pig at the time. The position as truffle hog should be altered."

"If you wish, Captain." Truffles sighed.

"Surely he has his sea legs now. Sausage, get down from there. We are changing positions!" the captain shouted. Captain Bacon scratched his chin thoughtfully. "Tusk," he said, pointing toward the fierce pirate. "Go up and give

it a try." After a few minutes, Captain Bacon shook his head, seeing him in the boar's nest. "Tusk, you're too much of a porker. Get down from there! Curly, what is taking so long?" Bacon asked, seeing that he was no more than ten snouts away from the boar's nest.

"I'm scared of any height beyond thirty-one snouts high," he said, gripping the mast for dear life.

"Fine, get down from there! Pickles!" Captain Bacon shouted. After a few minutes, he shook his head in disbelief. "I don't even want to know," Bacon said, seeing Pickles waving in the wind, his earring attached to the pirate flag.

"Sausage, you might as well get back up into the boar's nest for now," Captain Bacon said thoughtfully.

Who could possibly be a truffle hog? Captain Bacon wondered before glancing at Truffles.

"Captain Bacon! Captain Bacon!" Sausage yelled from the boar's nest.

"Speak, Sausage!" he shouted, looking up at him.

"The ship on the edge of the Albatross Sea is huge and well designed."

"Do you know what it is?"

"It is designed with horns and shields. There is a baby bottle on the flag. I can't tell what the ship's called, but it's *Sea*-something."

"See? See, what? What do you see?"

"I don't know what I see, but it is named *Sea* . . . I can't tell what the other half is—*Sea Monster, Sea Serpent, Sea Horse, Sea Saw?*" Sausage guessed.

"You've got super sucky sight, Sausage!" Captain Bacon call. "Keep an eye out for what that ship is called. I want to know it the minute you figure out what its name is."

Bacon then turned toward his first mate. "I am going to see what type of ship that is, while you keep a slow course toward that ship."

"Aye, Captain!" his first mate said before following his orders.

Captain Bacon went into his quarters and placed a heavy book of flags on his desk before he began searching the pages. He saw it right there, on page 24. A baby bottle is the symbol for cows. One thing Captain Bacon knew is that all cattle that sail are known as the Vikings of the Albatross Sea.

There was another knock at his door.

"Enter," the captain said before Truffles walked in.

Sausage has more information on the ship. The moment Bacon stepped out, Sausage called down to him.

"Captain! Captain! Its name is the *Sea Cow*! Not the sea monster! The *Sea Cow*!"

Captain Bacon rubbed his chin. "I see. Tusk!" Captain Bacon shouted.

"No! Not Tusk cows!" Sausage corrected.

"Silence, Sausage. I'm calling Tusk."

The tough wild boar stormed up from the pigpen below deck.

"Yes, Captain?"

"Prepare your plungers. We have some Viking cattle to herd."

"What have they heard?" Tusk asked. "I heard you and Sausage."

"They heard nothing."

"But I heard you," Tusk said, confused.

"Forget what you heard!" Captain Bacon shouted, frustrated.

"What should I forget to hear?"

Captain Bacon took a deep breath, calming himself. "Prepare to raid some Vikings. We have them in our sights."

"Aye, Captain," Tusk said before alerting the crew below deck.

Har! Snort! Harg! Captain Bacon laughed excitedly. "Full speed ahead, Truffles! We need more sails released to go faster." Captain Bacon turned around, spotting a pig looking at their target. "Curly! Raise the sails! Sausage!"

he shouted, turning to the runt. "Replace the plunger flag for a baby bottle!"

"You bet!" he said in the boar's nest.

"Aye, Captain Bacon!" Curly said before climbing the ropes to untie more sails.

As the sails unraveled, Tusk and Pickles secured them.

"We attack!" Captain Bacon shouted, pulling his plunger from its covering and pointing it at the ship.

"Captain?" Truffles said slowly.

"Silence! I am looking forward to this attack."

"But, Captain . . ."

"What? Can't you see I am filled with relish?"

"Excuse me, Captain Bacon?" his first mate asked, confused.

"I'm relishing in my feelings!" Truffles still looked at his captain confused. "My excitement and joy of another ship is guiding us toward the *Sea Cow*!" Captain Bacon explained even more.

"I am sorry, Captain, but with my guessing on wind speed, sea current, and your relish-filled feelings, we will reach the cattle ship in about three or four hours."

"WHAT? I can't wait another hour! By then, my relish will run out."

Truffles stared at Captain Bacon, unsure what to say.

"Don't look at me like that. I haven't been in the cucumbers," Captain Bacon said before storming toward his pen. "By the way," Captain Bacon said, turning around, "we shall eat supper in one hour. I don't want anyone to have any stomach pains when we are raiding the *Sea Cow* Vikings. I will be in my quarters, writing in my ship's log."

CHAPTER 4

Bacon's Log

Today we have a ship on the horizon. But it's not a normal ship. It's a Viking ship that we are going to raid. Cows always think they are so tough with their leather jackets, but guess what, I, Captain Bacon, am the most feared pirate on the Albatross Sea. We will outwit them with our pork-chop ability.

Cattle Ship's Information
How to identify: Baby bottle, big, bulky, and built for defense
Ship's advantage: Average
Best way of approach: Fast and quiet
Possible inventory: Milk; paint brushes; black, white, or brown leather jackets; tennis rackets; fire extinguishers

Closing the ship's log, Captain Bacon walked toward his ham-mock. A short nap before supper and then we attack! Captain Bacon thought

as he started an egg timer before jumping into his ham-mock to catch some winks and snorts. Covering himself in a wool blanket, he closed his eyes. Listening to the ticking sound of his egg timer and the rocking motion of the ship, slowly, Captain Bacon began to snore and snort deep in his dreams.

"Captain Bacon!" Truffles shouted as he ran into the captain's quarters.

Frightened, Captain Bacon jumped five snouts high before landing on the floor.

"Truffles! What have I told you about busting into my quarters without knocking?"

"Nothing, sir. You haven't said anything about that."

"Well, remind me to yell at you later. Right now, I want to know, why did you dare disrupt my sleep? I was out like a pig."

"We have reached the Manatee."

"Manatee? I thought the ship was called the *Sea Cow*."

Truffles raised an eyebrow. "Is there a difference?"

"If it's not the actual name on the ship, then yes! It would be like calling you mushroom."

"I apologize, Captain."

"And?" he asked, wanting more information. "Is there anything else?"

"Yes, Captain," Truffles said, grinning. "I also wanted to tell you the Sea Cow is ours, and as we drew near, we saw the cows jump the fence."

Getting up off the floor, Captain Bacon looked at Truffles, confused. "What does that mean? I have to see this for myself."

Bacon's crew of pork belly pirates cheered as he walked onto the deck. Looking at the ship floating next to them, Captain Bacon walked onto the cattle ship. On the horizon, Captain Bacon could see the crew rowing away. Captain Bacon turned around to face his wormy crew of pirates.

"I declare the *Sea Cow* in the name of Captain Bacon! We won!"

His crew cheered at their grand victory when, suddenly, a shout came from the *Squealer*. "Captain Bacon! Captain Bacon!"

The crew's cheers were suddenly silenced as Sausage in the boar's nest shouted, pointing out to sea, "Tattered sails are coming!"

Captain Bacon dashed in the direction Sausage was pointing, seeing the creaky ship sailing toward them. Captain Bacon stared frozen, stiff as he watched a cannon fire at him.

Crack! The object hit him in the head, knocking him flat on the deck. Unable to move, Captain Bacon lay there, his head pounding and a maddening ringing in his ears.

"Ugg! What hit me?" Captain Bacon asked himself as he opened his eyes.

A deafening ringing made it hard to think as he looked up at the ceiling of his quarters. Relief waved over him, knowing they weren't going to be invaded. Looking over his shoulder, he saw the egg timer ringing on the floor next to him.

Shutting off the timer, he felt his forehead.

"Ouch!" Bacon grunted, feeling his head. "Not a good day!" Captain Bacon decided, sitting up from the floor as anger suddenly started to set in.

Even though the egg timer was the size of a chicken's egg, Captain Bacon had a goose egg on his forehead. Getting up off the floor, he stared at his twisted ham-mock angrily. *All that loot we ended up gathering, and—poof!—it was all a dream.* Untwisting his ham-mock, Captain

Bacon threw his wool blanket on his bed before storming out on deck.

"Hello, Captain . . ." Truffles stopped in midsentence. "Are you all right? That looks like it—"

"Silence, Truffles! I didn't wake up on the right side of the ham-mock," the captain said, going down below deck.

At the pigpen, Captain Bacon walked past the sleeping pirates as he headed lower into the potbelly of the *Squealer*. Reaching the mess hall, Captain Bacon sat down, waiting for a bowl of slop and a plate of apple cores on the side. Captain Bacon's chef Pepperoni turned around, holding the captain's order.

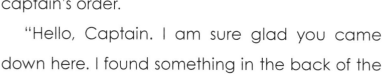

"Hello, Captain. I am sure glad you came down here. I found something in the back of the pantry."

"You mean in the piggy bank?" Captain Bacon corrected.

"Yes, Captain." Pepperoni looked around the room, seeing Tusk gobbling food. "They may be stale, but I know that is how you like them."

"Stale? What did you find that I like stale? I don't even like the word 'stale.' Because I am a pig pirate, the word I like is 'rich.' Tell me, Pepper, what is it?"

Pepperoni glanced at Tusk before leaning in to whisper to Captain Bacon. "I found some doughnuts," she said.

"Well, what do you think we should do with them?" Tusk asked, standing right over Captain Bacon's shoulder.

"How?" Bacon asked, looking at the boar warrior.

"I may be a muscle head, but I have ears like an elephant," Tusk said thoughtfully. "Actually, it's more like the ears of a bat. Elephant ears are kind of big." Captain Bacon and Pepperoni looked at Tusk for a moment, stunned. "Unless you are talking about the pastry called elephant ears, those are really good, especially if you put icing sugar and applesauce on it because apples are the tastiest things on this ship," Tusk squealed with delight.

"What are you talking about, Tusk?" Captain Bacon asked.

Tusk looked at the two of them, confused. "Aren't we talking about apples?" Captain Bacon and Pepperoni shook their heads slowly. "I apologize. I am just sleepy from our paper-diaper raid, and I'm also excited about the new ship that we will be reaching in ten minutes."

"Prepare the others and your plungers, cattle ships have a great defense."

"Aye, Captain," Tusk said before turning to leave. "Paper, diapers," Tusk muttered as he left.

⚓

"That pig's attention span surprises me every day," Pepper said. "Last night he went from talking about the Robin's Hood to what made plungers magically sticky to hoof clippers."

"At least he is a good boar warrior and that he is on our side."

Pepperoni nodded before heading behind the serving counter and picking up a white box of stale doughnuts.

"That looks mightily good. We will celebrate with this once the piggy bank is full of loot. For the moment, I will put it in my private piggy bank."

"I remember now!" Tusk declared, standing at the stairs to the mess hall. Tusk walked right up to Pepper and Captain Bacon. "I remember what you were talking about before I got sidetracked with something."

"It was apples," Pepperoni reminded Tusk.

"Right! I remember that now! My favorite is Granny's. She picks all her green apples from her orchard. You know, I don't get to talk to her often since she moved out of the city. Living in that big red brick house in the country, I worry about all the wolves she has as neighbors."

"Aye, wolves can be a real pain, but do you know what else is?" Captain Bacon asked Tusk.

"Walking into a room and not remembering why you went in there in the first place?" he guessed.

Captain Bacon stared at Tusk as if he couldn't believe he just answered Captain Bacon that quickly. "Yes. But that wasn't the answer I was looking for."

"Oh. I know. I know what the real answer is. Well, actually, only you know the answer, but I can guess. It is a real pain when we raid ships and there isn't anything of real worth on them."

"I have to go, Captain," Pepper said, heading back into the kitchen.

"Yes. That is a real pain, but that isn't what I wanted to hear," Captain Bacon said, getting annoyed.

"What is it then?" Tusk asked.

"What I find a pain is that we are approaching the Sea Cow and you are in the mess hall playing fifty questions!"

"The Sea Cow! Right! I will go right now!" Tusk said before charging up the stairs.

Captain Bacon took a deep breath before going up the stairs with the box of stale doughnuts. Reaching to the pigpen, Captain Bacon saw Pickles and Curly playing checkers.

"Get on deck! Don't you know we are about to raid a ship?" Captain Bacon squealed.

Surprised, both of the potbellied buccaneers grabbed their plungers before dashing up onto the deck. Captain Bacon walked onto the deck, looking at the Squealer's next victim.

The cattle ship was wide and tall. Unlike the guard rails on Captain Bacon's ship, the Sea Cow had two lines of barbwire nailed onto posts. All the shields hanging on the side of the ship had the baby bottle symbol on them.

Captain Bacon lifted his plunger in the air. "Harg!" he shouted.

Instantly, the rest of the pirate crew began *harg*-ing along. The cattle crew came to the side of the *Sea Cow* to look at the plunger-prepared pig pirates.

"Prepare for an unplanned plunger and plunder from the professional pig pirates!" Captain Bacon shouted.

The herd stood near the barbwire fence, watching Captain Bacon and his crew of pirates in the suddenly very awkward silence. Captain Bacon glance at Truffles, confused with their unusual reaction. After a few awkward minutes of silence staring at each other, Captain Bacon glanced at Truffles who silently shrugged. The *Squealer*'s crew glanced at Captain Bacon, wondering what would happen next. Apart from waves hitting the side of the ships, all was silent.

Captain Bacon looked at the curious crew above them.

"Attack!" Captain Bacon shouted, raising his plunger toward the ship.

On Captain Bacon's command, cannons below deck fired at the *Sea Cow*.

CHAPTER 5

The *Sea Cow*'s crew vanished as giant plungers stuck to the side of the *Sea Cow*, keeping them attached to the *Squealer* as the crew fired ropes tied to plungers toward the ship. Placing the box of doughnuts on the deck, Captain Bacon and his crew climbed aboard.

Aboard the *Sea Cow*, Captain Bacon shouted at the cattle, "My name is Captain Bacon, and as of right now, I own your ship. Tusk! Curly! Go search the ship and see if you can find anything up in the cow nest."

"Actually, it's called a hayloft," Curly said.

"Fine, Curly, search the hayloft. Tusk, search the food silos and the underbelly."

"You mean the udder?" Truffles asked.

Bacon stared at him as silence filled the air. "Yes, look udder there."

Suddenly, the door to the captain's quarters opened. Captain Bacon turned around and looked up at a black and white Holstein cow.

"Why hello! What are you supposed to be, an oversized Dalmatian?"

"Funny. I am Bessie, captain of this vessel. What are you, a sausage roll?"

"How dare you!" Captain Bacon shouted. "I am Captain Bacon, the terror of the Albatross Sea. I am to be feared." The pig captain sucked in his stomach, making himself stand taller and a little bit less potbellied.

"Fear me!" Bessie looked at her crew. "Daisy, please start routine fifty for these pink bellies."

"Aye, Captain Bessie," Daisy, a brown cow, said before turning toward the crew.

"Routine? What do you mean 'routine'? What is a 'routine'?"

"Iceberg ahead!" Daisy shouted, making all the cattle rush to the front of the ship to look overboard."

"What? It's the middle of summer. There are no icebergs."

Captain Bessie shook her head. "Daisy! I said routine fifty, not fifteen! Five-zero."

"I understand that now. I am sorry, Captain," Daisy said, shyly stepping back. "I didn't think there were icebergs out there."

Captain Bessie turned toward Captain Bacon. "To answer your question about routine, it is something that you do normally."

"I know what a routine is, but why are they numbered?" Bacon shouted.

"There is no need to shout. I can hear you quite clearly. Our routines are used in case something gets in our way."

"You don't give the orders around here! I do!"

Bessie shook her head. "You may be the captain of your ship, but I am the head of the herd here. They will only listen to me," Bessie said sternly.

"Does not a candle cry tears of wax as he sits on the table watching the chandelier sway and dance above him?"

"I . . ." Captain Bacon froze, confused from the

sudden outburst from the crew member. "Is there something wrong with him? Is he some sort of crazy, mad cow? That didn't make any sense."

"He is Sir Tenderloin, the poet of our ship."

"Poet? Why don't we have a poet, Truffles?" Bacon asked his first mate.

"You said that they are annoying and that they are constantly snapping their hooves whenever they read their rhymes."

"It sounds like something I would say. I don't like being snapped at," Captain Bacon said, nodding.

"As a manatee is a gentle beast of the ocean, does that mean that an actual sea cow that rides the waves be as gentle as waves at the beach," Sir Tenderloin said, his right hoof snapping to a makeshift rhythm.

Bacon glared at Truffles, annoyed.

"Did I say something wrong?" his first mate asked.

"Tusk! Is there anything in the udder belly?" Captain Bacon shouted down into the ship.

"They have just a couple of leather jackets and a few fire extinguishers . . . Hey . . ."

"You found hay?"

"No, straw."

"Then why are you shouting 'hay'?"

"I said, 'hey,' as in I just found some green onions, apples, and peas! Did you know that if you find four peas in a pod, it is considered a family? And they all have their own names. There's Green Pea, Snow Pea, Black-eyed Pea, and Sweet Pea. I think of the *Squealer* as our own peapod. And we are a big family. Do you ever think of us as a big happy—"

"That's enough, Tusk. Gather the apples and jackets and come up here."

"Aye, Captain Bacon," Tusk said.

"Soon we will have your loot and be off."

"Here you go, Captain," First Mate Daisy said, placing an empty barrel on deck.

"I don't think I asked for a barrel, but thank you," Bacon said.

"This is so great! Chickens and cows being raided by pigs. Now all we need to do is find a sheep liner and we will have a complete farmers' market."

"You are out of season for them," a bull snorted. "Sheep ships ship their products in winter. Lotions and winter coats don't sell well in summer."

Captain Bacon turned around, seeing the longest set of horns he had ever seen. "And if this were my ship, we would hog tie you and toss you back where you came from," he said angrily.

"Oh! Well, it's my ship, so lucky me."

Captain Bacon said proudly, "Let me guess, you are from Texas?" The pig captain smirked.

"Actually, it's Chicago," he replied.

Suddenly, Captain Bacon felt lifted off the ground. "HEEEEE!" Captain Bacon squealed in surprise. "Oh my ham!" he moaned, landing in the empty barrel.

Stunned, Captain Bacon suddenly realized what happened. When his back was turned, Captain Bessie kicked him in the hind quarters.

"Tusk! Pickles! Curly! Plunger them all!" Bacon shouted as he looked over the rim of the barrel. "That is the last time you will—eeeek!" Captain Bacon ducked into the wooden barrel as Bessie put her head down and charged.

Thump! The barrel landed on its side. Bessie put her head against the side of the barrel, shoving him around like a barrel of monkeys.

"Stop it! This is mutiny!" Captain Bacon shouted as he suddenly realized he was getting rolled

right off the ship. "Heeeeeeeelp!" he shouted. Captain Bacon felt weightless for a moment.

Thud! "Oooh, my ham hurts," Captain Bacon said, rubbing his rear before looking up at the two ships. "Sausage!" he shouted up at the *Squealer*'s boar's nest. "He must be asleep again."

Captain Bacon reached into his pocket, pulling out his slingshot. He suddenly realized he didn't have any pebbles to fire. *That's useless to me*, he thought, putting it back in his pocket.

Splash! Captain Bacon saw Tusk treading water.

"Captain!" Tusk said, surprised. "Why did you get a barrel and I didn't?" he asked, bobbing in the water.

Captain Bacon rolled his eyes. "I am the captain of the ship. That is why I was given a barrel."

"That makes sense . . . It also makes sense that the world isn't flat because the Albatross Sea would dry up when it fell off the edge of the world. Speaking off all dried up—"

"Silence, Tusk. Let's just get back on the *Squealer* and figure out what went wrong," Captain Bacon said as he used his plunger to row back to his ship.

"Hieeeee!"

Captain Bacon and Tusk looked up as Curly flew over their heads before landing in the sea. Suddenly, another pig pirate and another came flying over their heads.

"My mother would be completely squeak-less if she knew pigs were flying," Tusk said, amazed.

"Silence!" Captain Bacon shouted. "Return to the *Squealer*. They have won this round, but I, Captain Bacon, never forgets a foe!"

Suddenly, another pig flew over the fence, splashing right in front of Captain Bacon, making his barrel bob in the water.

"YOU MISSED!" Captain Bacon shouted, laughing. *Har! Snort! Harg!*

"Cow pie at six-o-clock—or is that twelve?" Pickles shouted.

"Six-o-clock is behind you, twelve is—"

Splat! The cow pie hit Captain Bacon right in the face.

The cow crew bellowed with victory. Captain Bacon removed the pie pan off his head.

"That was twelve-o-clock."

Suddenly, a cowbell rang. "Dinner!"

Captain Bacon carefully tipped his floating barrel until he could wash his face off. "I won't forget this!" Captain Bacon shouted as he stood up. "We will return! And we will be victorious!" Captain Bacon looked to his wet, wild hog crew.

"Return to the *Squealer*. The next time our ships cross, we know what routine fifty is."

"Captain, I think—"

"Silence, Tusk, we must focus on returning to my ship. Then you can tell me about your family."

"But, Captain, our ship is sailing away! But now that you mentioned it, did I ever tell you about how my half-wit brother got stranded on a rowboat?"

Captain Bacon turned his attention toward the *Squealer* sailing away as Tusk continued his story. "As your captain, return this instant!" Captain Bacon shouted as his chubby pink face turned tomato red.

The *Squealer*'s cannon plungers were still attached to the side of the *Sea Cow* as the nearly crewless pirate ship was being slowly towed away from the overboard boars. Pulling out his plunger, Captain Bacon began using it as he paddled as fast as he could. Suddenly, Sausage looked over the boar's nest.

"Hey!" Captain Bacon shouted, suddenly waving his plunger in the air.

Sausage suddenly spotted the pirate crew treading water behind the *Squealer*. *We're in luck!* Captain Bacon thought. Suddenly, Sausage waved back before climbing over the side of the nest and down the ropes near the mast.

"This isn't going to end well," Truffles said, treading water near Captain Bacon.

Sausage flew over the edge of the ship. "HEEEEE!" Sausage squealed in surprise as he fell overboard.

"Yup, you can't depend on him. That lump of lard is useless when he's out of the boar's nest."

Quickly, Captain Bacon reached Sausage treading water.

"Somebody left a box of doughnuts on deck, and I tripped on them. By the way, falling off

the ship is normally my curse. Why are you guys overboard?" Sausage asked.

"Bah. The herd hit us when our rumps were turned."

"Well, how are we going to get up on deck?" Sausage asked.

"I believe we may need the help of our secret weapon," the captain said, shaking his head. "You're not suggesting on calling . . ."

"We have to do something, or else, we will have more to worry about other than the ship with tattered sails."

"Right as usual, Captain Bacon," Truffles said. "Captain, sir, look."

"No, I am too upset. Don't you know, if we call the secret weapon, we will be helpless against either the Robin's Hood or the tattered sails."

"You don't have to call her. Look," Sausage said.

Captain Bacon looked up at their ship, spotting a pig on deck. *Well, who could that be?* Captain Bacon wondered. They watched the pig vanished from the deck, and within a minute, the plungers popped off the *Sea Cow*, landing in the water.

"Aye! Head for the ship's plungers! We have been salvaged."

"Salvaged? What is 'salvaged'?" Tusk asked.

"It means your raisin rump is saved."

"Yay! I'm saved!" Tusk cheered, splashing around. "I'll come back and save you all as soon as I can."

The entire crew groaned. "We are all getting rescued, squirrel brain, not just you."

"Oh. I thought it was just me, like the time I fell in a well and my brother had to leave for half an hour to find rope."

"Captain, shall I give him a dunk?" First Mate Truffles asked.

Captain Bacon shook his head before turning to Tusk who hadn't even stopped talking to take a breath. Taking his plunger, Captain Bacon placed the plunger on his head, dunking him underwater. A mass of bubbles rose to the surface seconds before Tusk's head reappeared.

"You know, right after my brother Pinky rescued me from the well, he pushed me back in. He said I talked too much, but shortly after that, he pulled me out of the well again."

Captain Bacon stared at him in disbelief. How can someone talk so much about nothing?

"Captain!" Sausage shouted.

"What now?"

"Look! Ship on the horizon!"

"You can't be serious!" Captain Bacon exclaimed.

Captain turned to look at the new ship. It was hard to tell what ship it was near the setting sun.

"Come on, crew, we are close enough to reach," Captain Bacon said as he used his plunger and began rowing toward the ship.

Reaching the *Squealer*, the pirates climbed up the giant plungers.

"Who on the Albatross Sea was on board to save us?" Pickles asked the crew.

"For your information, that would be me," a pig said, leaning against the door of the pigpen.

"Pepperoni?" Tusk exclaimed. "But you're just a cook!"

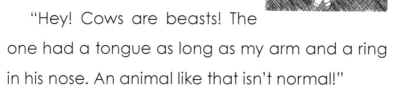

"Just a cook! That sounds funny coming from someone who got their butt kicked by a cow."

"Hey! Cows are beasts! The one had a tongue as long as my arm and a ring in his nose. An animal like that isn't normal!"

"Anyway, let's give Pepper a cheer for saving us," Captain Bacon declared.

Harr! Snort! Harrrr! The entire crew *harg-ed* and snorted a cheer.

"I better get back up to the boar's nest just in case I fall overboard again," Sausage said before he stared heading toward the rigging near the mast.

SPLASH! "Sausage splashed on the portside," Truffles said.

"HELP!" Sausage shouted from below.

While the crew looked overboard at Sausage, Captain Bacon looked out toward the setting sun at the ship. *Is it my imagination, or is the ship sailing toward us?* Captain Bacon wondered.

"Thank you," Sausage said as he hung tightly to the wooden railing.

"Tusk, take Sausage to the rafters and make sure he makes it to the boar's nest."

Tusk grabbed the back of Sausage's shirt, pulling him back onto the ship.

"Whoa!" *Splash!* "Help!" Tusk shouted, splashing.

Sausage froze in place before daring to look over his shoulder. A massive grin spread across his face. "THE CURSE IS BROKEN!" Sausage shouted, jumping from one foot to the other excitedly. "I'll never fall off the ship again!"

"Great. Now get up to the boar's nest before you fall overboard again," Truffles said, unimpressed.

"Aye, yes, sir!" Sausage said before rushing up the rafters to the boar's nest.

"Sausage!" Captain Bacon shouted. "What can you tell me about the ship on the horizon?"

"I can't tell. It's too far away to tell," Sausage replied, leaning over the barrier, trying to tell what kind of ship it was.

"Use your spyglass!" Captain Bacon shouted before looking at Tusk as he climbed on deck.

Taking a couple of deep gasping breaths, Tusk stared angrily at Sausage. "How dare you shove me overboard?" Tusk shook an angry hoof at him. "You better hope that was an accident!"

"That's enough," Captain Bacon said, quieting Tusk. "Now go below deck and get dried off. There's something about that ship in the distance that I don't trust."

Sausage searched the ship with his spyglass. "There's too much fog around it," he proclaimed. "I can't tell what kind of ship it is."

"Alert us if that ship continues to get closer."

Captain Bacon walked into his quarters, closing the door behind him. Captain Bacon sat behind his large desk and rubbed his eyes before turning on the lamp next to him.

Bacon's Log

Today was crazy. The crafty cattle crew kicked us off the *Sea Cow's* deck. And they had leather jackets! Perhaps it's for the best. There is a ship sailing near us, and it seems to be coming closer. Perhaps it's a ship that as yet knows not the wrath of the pork pirate Captain Bacon. Perhaps I should see how the potbellied crew is taking the streak of poor luck.

Closing Bacon's Log, Captain Bacon stepped out onto deck.

"Truffles, have you figured out whose ship is that bobbing in the distance?"

"No, and Sausage, up in the boar's nest, can't tell either."

"Very well," Captain Bacon said, walking toward the stairs.

Clump! Thump! Clump! Thump! As he walked down the stairs into the pigpen, he heard the crew laughing so hard they were snorting. The captain froze, listening in on what they were saying.

"You didn't see this, but when we were raiding the *Beaker*, a chicken called Henrietta hit me with a throw pillow," Curly said. "It wasn't until that moment that I realized, I was allergic to chicken feathers."

"How did you figure that out?" Pickles asked.

"It was easy. A chicken feather went up my nose when it hit me. After that, I couldn't stop sneezing until it flew out of my nose. Even now, my right nose hole tickles."

"Oh! Come on! You're not allergic to chicken feathers. It's the same as when you were up in the hayloft of the *Sea Cow* and you told me you got a fever from the hay because you were getting hot and sweaty. Little did you realize it was just a really hot room," Pickles shouted, making everyone snort.

"That's nothing!" Tusk shouted over the snorts. "On the *Sea Cow*, I saw a bull that had a ring in his nose and a piercing in each ear. He chased me up the stairs onto the deck. Next thing I knew, he lifted me off the ground, and I was sitting on his head. It was a real rodeo before he bunted me over the barbwire, which, by the way, reminds me of a crazed pig I met back in New Hampshire, with a barbwire tattoo all the way around his stomach."

Captain Bacon stepped the rest of the way down the steps, and suddenly, everything became quiet.

Clump! Thump! Clump! Thump! He looked at his tired crew lying in their ham-mocks.

"There is a ship out on the starboard side."

The entire crew moaned.

"What? Are you a pile of baby backs? We must defend the *Squealer*!"

"Aye, aye, Captain!" Tusk shouted as he leaned on one of the cannons.

Rolling away from him, Tusk stumbled before falling out of the port window into the sea.

SPLASH!

"Hog overboard!" he shouted, landing in the water. "Help me!"

Captain Bacon and Pickles hurried up onto the deck. Pickles pulled out his bow and plunger attached to a rope as he took the steps, two at a time, up to the deck. Looking over the edge of the port bow, he steadied his aim and fired the plunger at the boar warrior. Hitting him right on the top of the head, Pickles gripped the rope. Pulling him back up onto the deck, Tusk spoke up quickly. "Give me a spyglass,"

he said quickly. Pickles handed him one. Tusk spun around, looking right at the ship covered in fog. "They have tattered sails," Tusk declared.

A shiver went through the captain like a slice of bacon on a hot frying pan.

BLUNDER

CHAPTER 6

"Sausage! Is it true, are they tattered sails?"

"I can't tell! No matter how I turn the spyglass, they're too far for me to tell."

"Truffles! Turn the ship, we are getting out of here."

"Where are we heading?" he asked.

"I don't care as long as we stay away from that ship," the captain said, pointing toward the ship.

"Captain, permission to change positions with Sausage up in the boar's nest. I have a feeling that I have this so-called curse of falling head over ham off the ship," Tusk said.

"No," the captain declared. "You are my best warrior. I need you to defend my crew if that ship overtakes us. And curses aren't real unless you believe them, and I don't believe in them."

"But I do. To a degree. You see, my grandmother on my grandfather's side—"

"You no longer believe in curses. That is an order."

"Yes, Captain!" Tusk said, saluting the captain before turning and stepping away.

Not paying attention to where he was going, Tusk walked into the fence. Flipping over the ship's barrier, Tusk fell into the water.

"I just told you to stop believing in curses!" he shouted down to the soggy hog.

"I apologize, Captain Bacon! Please help me up."

"Pickles, pull him out and be quick about it. We are getting out of here."

Captain Bacon turned on his hoof and walked into his quarters. Concerned, he stared at his ham-mock. His nightmare was coming true.

Captain Bacon sighed, shaking his head. Tossing his hat on to the ham-mock, he walked toward his desk. He glanced at the other side of his room, seeing himself in a full-length mirror. He started the day chasing chickens and ended running from bulls. Today wasn't a good day, but it doesn't mean it will end badly. He couldn't help but feel like he had gained a couple more wraps of bacon around his middle. Holding his stomach, he stood straighter, trying to look more official.

"I am the captain. I have a loyal drove that is willing to do anything I say. We will avoid this!"

The captain walked toward his desk and slammed his hoof on top, making everything shake on his desk. He looked at his Bacon's

Log, grinning. Then the next moment, his desk collapsed into dozens of pieces.

"Are you kidding me?" he shouted in disgust.

What could Pickles be possibly be doing with all these nails? He turned toward the door, storming toward it. He kicked it open. Rather than swinging open, it collapsed onto the deck in pieces. He stood frozen. He couldn't see anything past his short stubby arms. They were surrounded by thick fog that began rolling into his quarters.

"Truffles!" Captain Bacon shouted into the silent fog.

After a few moments of silence, he pulled out his plunger and slowly walked toward the direction of the helm. Walking through the fog to the helm revealed nothing. Truffles was gone. Bacon swung his plunger around, behind him, expecting to find someone. Not feeling anything with his plunger, he steadily walked toward the

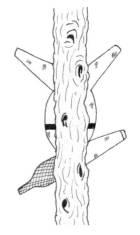

mast. Perhaps Sausage knows something. The captain walked in the general direction of the wooden pole. *Thump.* He grabbed his flat nose after he walked into it.

"Sausage! Are you there?" he shouted before pulling out his slingshot.

Aiming it upward, he guessed where the boar's nest was. No thud, no squeal, not hearing Sausage above him. *Thump.* The pebble came down, hitting him in the middle of his bald head. He looked back thinking about getting his hat, but he couldn't leave his crew wherever they were. Perhaps they are down below. Arms outstretched, he walked toward the door to the pigpen. Reaching the door, he stepped in, heading below deck. Fog following at his heels, he looked around the lower deck, seeing his entire crew hiding under wool blankets.

"Get out from under there!" Captain Bacon shouted at his crew. "You're fearless pirates, not frightened pigs in a blanket! Step up and let's defend what we have. We will not go down like a litter of runts." Truffles stepped up, coming from the mess hall. "The captain is right for once," he said, eating an apple. "We need to defend our ship and hide—I mean, fight behind our captain and for our captain."

Sausage cheered quietly.

"Well, you have me," Peperoni said, coming up from the mess hall. "And we have our secret weapon sleeping down in the hold. Who's behind our captain?" Peperoni asked.

"I am," said Pickles, followed by Sausage again.

"I will follow you to the edge of the earth," Tusk said.

Slowly, the entire crew stood up and joined their captain.

"Everyone, prepare!" the captain shouted. "We may not make it out of this fight with our ship intact," Captain Bacon said as every crew member held up their plungers.

Together, they followed their captain up the stairs toward the open deck. Shoulder to shoulder, Captain Bacon and his crew stood in a circle around the mast, waiting. Captain Bacon scratched his bald head, realizing he didn't have his hat on.

"Sausage, you like following my orders," Bacon said.

"Yes, Captain," Sausage said, sounding a little nervous.

"Go into the captain's mess and grab my hat. And watch yourself that you don't fall overboard."

"Yes, Captain," Sausage said, feeling a little uneasy in the fog. Walking in one direction, he grabbed the pig scout.

"My pen is over there," Bacon said, turning Sausage around.

The sound of ripping sails could be heard. They were close . . . too close. A moment later, Bacon saw something charging toward him. Captain Bacon pushed the plunger into the figure in the fog. In the silence, they heard the sound of the plunger's suction attach to the figure followed by a muffled scream. Pulling the plunger through the fog, Captain Bacon saw Sausage's face attached to the other end of the plunger.

"That was fast," Bacon said, surprised as he held the pirate hat in his hoof. "Tusk, help Sausage out," he said.

BAAAA! The crew heard the scream come from the other ship.

"Steady, pig snouts," Captain Bacon said as a pop echoed from the suctioned pig.

"Sorry for scaring you, Captain. It's scary out there in all that fog."

Slowly, the ship came into view through the fog. The sails were torn from being eaten. The sound of a horn being blown echoed around them.

"BAAAA!" the strange crew shouted.

"Steady!" Captain Bacon repeated.

A thud sounded as something landed on the deck. "BAAAA!" More of the strange crew jumped onto the *Squealer*.

"NOW!" Captain Bacon shouted.

The entire crew spread out onto the ship going after the invaders. Spotting one on deck, Captain

Bacon charged toward it. Standing on all four, Captain Bacon pressed the plunger against its forehead before looking at what he was attacking.

"A goat?" he said confused, looking at the creature. "They don't sail ships!"

Shaking its head, it pulled the plunger out of the captain's hands before hitting him with the handle of the suctioned stick.

"Back off, beast!" Captain Bacon shouted, stepping back from him shaking his head in every direction. Captain Bacon turned, running away from the assault as he thought about getting another plunger.

"Captain! They're goats!" Tusk shouted, running next to their leader.

Plunger-less, they ran down the side of the ship on their way to the door to the lower deck.

"We need more plungers!" Captain Bacon shouted to him.

"That's what I was thinking," Tusk said before vanishing in an instant.

Captain Bacon stopped to look behind himself to see that he was nowhere to be found. *SPLASH!* Looking over the fence, he saw the boar warrior treading water below. *BAAAA!* The captain spun around, seeing a goat standing there, staring at him before charging forward. Standing his ground, Captain Bacon leaned forward, staring at the goat. At the last moment, he grabbed the goat by the horns. Lifting the goat off the ground, he swung him over the edge. *BAAAAA! Splash!*

"Hi, Spooky," Tusk said to the goat.

BOOM! The captain ducked as one of the cannons fired a plunger overhead.

"AHHH!" Sausage screamed as he sailed overhead, his hoof tied to the giant plunger's rope.

SPLASH! "I need something to defend myself with, but maybe I should release my secret weapon before no one is on the ship to defend it."

"Captain!" Peperoni shouted to him. "I strongly suggest it is time to release her." The sound of ripping came from the sails. "They're starting to eat the sails!" she exclaimed.

"I agree," Captain Bacon said, taking a deep breath. Filling his lungs with as much air as possible, he shouted into the fog, "SUZIEEEEEEEEEEE!"

Captain Bacon's squeal pierced the thick fog, making everything seem to slow to a stop. Even the screams of the goats seemed to become silent. After a moment of silence, the ship began to rumble and vibrate. Unable to keep his balance, Captain Bacon fell on the deck, unable to stand the quacking and rocking the ship was doing. The goat screams became a lower murmur.

"Get ready!" Captain Bacon shouted. "You will regret the day I called the iron pig!" He laughed into the air, the sound of boards breaking as she stormed up from the belly of the ship.

The door burst open as five goats charged on deck, followed by a deafening squeal. The walls next to the door exploded as a two-thousand-  pound sow charged through where the door used to be.

Captain Bacon started to add up how much damage he was going to have to pay as the Poland China sow charged at the intruders.

"I'm not a goat!" Curly shouted just before landing in the water.

"BAAAA!" the goats started to scream louder as Suzie tossed everything in sight overboard.

Captain Bacon stayed still, letting the secret weapon run loose on the invaders. The sound of a horn echoed through the thick fog. The call on the goat's ship could be heard over the squeals and grunts of Suzie.

"What was that?" he asked, looking around in the fog.

"I think they are revealing their secret weapon," Truffles said, coming to the captain's right.

"Good old Suzie hasn't failed us yet," Captain Bacon said.

"Let's just hope we still have a ship after all this," Pepper added as a goat went flying off the ship, taking a part of the wooden barrier along with him.

The trio walked around the border of the ship, keeping the fence to their back as they looked out trying to find anyone else on deck, pig or goat. A creepy scream came from somewhere.

"What was that?" Pepper asked, swinging her plunger around.

Thump! A large goat landed on the deck, followed by another and another.

"What *is* that?" the three asked at the same time.

They looked like white outlines in the white fog. They were bigger than the first goats, but they were clearly still no match for Suzie. She charged toward them, making the ship rock from one side to another.

"They're afraid of her!" Captain Bacon exclaimed as they leaped away.

"I don't think so. They're coming right this way!" Truffles shouted, seeing them come right for them.

Unable to dive out of the way in time, they stood solid, awaiting their doom. Suddenly, the three white goats leaped over the pirate crew's head before standing on the edge of the fence. They looked down at the pigs grinning.

Confused, Captain Bacon suddenly realized what they were. "They're mountain goats!" he exclaimed as they suddenly dashed down the ridge of the ship.

WHAM! Captain Bacon, Pepper, and Truffles were slammed right off the ship by a two-thousand-pound secret weapon. Unconscious, Captain Bacon and the entire pirate crew floated in the water as the *Squealer* sailed away.

EPILOGUE

Captain Bacon forced a grunt as he opened his eyes. The sun was blinding as he lay on the sand. *What hit me?* he thought, his head pounding. Suddenly, it all came back to him: the tattered sails, the goats, and getting bowled over by Suzie. He sat up, looking at the endless ocean in front of an endless beach. *Am I dead? That's a shame. I never had the chance to get those pictures hung up in my pen again*, he thought to himself as he stood up. *If I am dead, this is a disappointment. I expected a lot more slop and mud.*

Thud!

Captain Bacon squealed in pain as a coconut hit him on the head.

"Apparently, I'm not dead, and this can't be a dream because that hurt too much," he said before throwing the coconut toward the waves.

Stretching his back, he felt a snap, crackle, and pop come from his pork ribs. He looked around, spotting Truffles giving orders. As if on cue, the first mate turned around, seeing the captain staring at him.

"Hello, Captain," he said, saluting him. He was holding a handful of papers. "I am so sorry, Captain," Truffles said, looking over their captain.

"What for?" he asked. "It isn't your fault we were bowled overboard."

That's not why, sir. I've been . . . um . . .," Truffles stammered. "Since you were knocked out, the crew and I turned you over every once in a while to keep you well, and it appears we accidently fried your bacon."

"What?" Captain Bacon asked, confused, before looking down at his bright red sunburned stomach. "YOU!" he exclaimed. "You completely fried my pork rinds!" he shouted.

"I apologize again, Captain," Truffles said, taking a step back.

"*You* don't turn me over like I'm on a rotisserie! That's how I became fried! If you didn't want to drag me into the shade, you should have just covered me in banana leaves!"

"That mistake won't be made again," Truffles said assuredly as Captain Bacon touched his stomach.

Breaking his attention from his stomach, he looked at the papers Truffles was holding. "What is that?" he asked, pointing toward the papers. "Are those blueprints?"

"Well, sort of . . .," Truffles said awkwardly.

"Give me, give me, give me," the captain said, ripping the pages out of his first mate's

hoof. "Are you building another ship?" he asked, quickly skimming it over.

"The crew believes that our fifth ship is going to be the golden raider," Truffles said, filling him in.

"I guess they'll need a captain then," Bacon said, rubbing his hooves together. "Is there anything else that I need to know, Truffles?" he asked his first mate.

"We found your books on land when we started snorting around."

"My books?" he asked, confused.

"This blueprint came from the goats' ship, along with your animal dictionary, ship flags, everything."

"Seriously? Take me to it," Captain Bacon ordered.

They walked past their working crew. Captain Bacon was guided past some thick bushes into an opening.

"By the way," Truffles said, "we are very fortunate that Pickles somehow found a ton of nails. I don't know where they came from, but we have enough to rebuild the ship."

"I can make a guess," Bacon grumbled to himself as they approached a clearing.

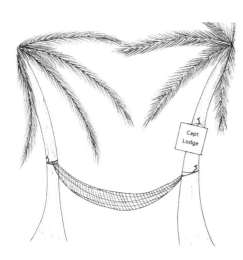

A ham-mock was attached to two trees. A sign read "Captain's Lodge" was nailed to the tree. Captain Bacon glared at the hanging sign for a moment before seeing a box next to his ham-mock. Walking to it, he found a note taped to the top of it. Lying in the shade of his tree, he read the note:

> Dear Captain Bacon,
> We may have taken your ship,
> but we have our reasons.
> We gave you back your books to prove
> we aren't completely baaaaad.
> Until next time we butt heads,
> Billy

Captain Bacon noticed that the signature was half eaten off the page. "I guess destiny is calling!"

"It's more like a note, sir," Truffles corrected.

"Fine," Bacon said, sighing. "Destiny is writing us.

Beaker

COW VIKINGS

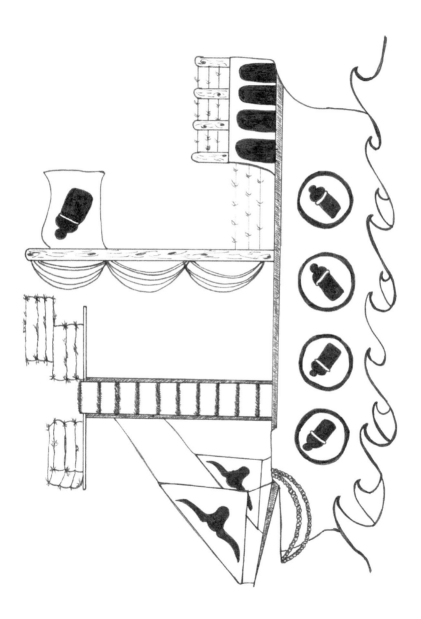

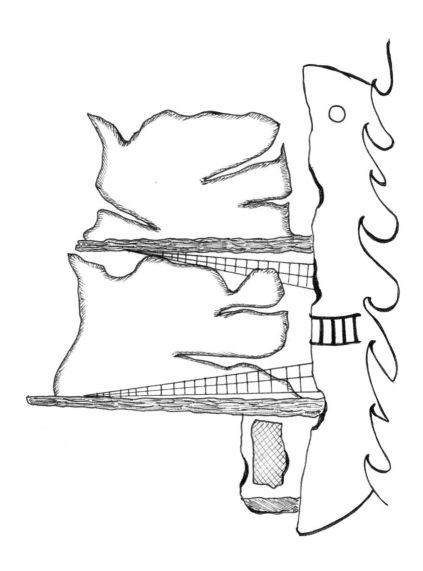

CPSIA information can be obtained
at www.ICGtesting.com
Printed in the USA
LVHW082114250919
632288LV00001B/1/P